PERIL O PLANET PELLIA

A Puzzle Planet Adventure

10/98

For Neil and Elizabeth
With love
M.B.

ORCHARD BOOKS
96 Leonard Street, London EC2A 4RH
Orchard Books Australia
14 Mars Road, Lane Cove, NSW 2066
First published in Great Britain 1996
First paperback publication 1997
Text © Oneta Malorie Blackman 1996
Illustrations © Patrice Aggs 1996
The right of Oneta Malorie Blackman to be identified as the Author
and Patrice Aggs as the Illustrator of this Work has been
asserted by them in accordance with the
Copyright, Designs and Patents Act, 1988.
A CIP catalogue record for this book is available
from the British Library.
1 85213 935 8 (hardback)
1 86039 371 3(paperback)
Printed in Great Britain.

Malorie Blackman

Illustrated by
Patrice Aggs

ORCHARD BOOKS

CONTENTS

Chapter

To the Rescue!

BLEEP! BLEEP! BLEEP! Zachary stuck his fingers in his ears. What a racket! That noise meant only one thing. Someone, somewhere, was in BIG trouble!

"CODE BLUE-TWELVE! CODE BLUE-TWELVE!"

Code blue-twelve was only used in real emergencies.

Zach ran over to his mum and dad's communicator – a state-of-the-art networked computer which allowed communication with other planets.

"Ready to receive," Zach spoke to the communicator.

"Mayday! Mayday! Zach, can you hear me?"

Intensely shocked, Zach recognised the voice. It was his best friend Emma. The communications channel crackled and hissed.

"Zach, can you hear me? I've crash-landed on Pellia. I don't think I'm on the ground. I'm not sure what I've crashed into... I...Oh no...Something's trying to get into my ship...Zach, help me. HELP ME..." Emma's voice broke off abruptly.

"Hi, Zach! What's going on?" Mum smiled as she strolled down the stairs.

"Mum, Emma's been taken prisoner on the planet Pellia," Zach could hardly get the words out.

Mum's smile vanished. She spoke directly to the communicator. "Computer, give me the details of Emma Cookson's last scheduled flight into space."

"Details are sketchy at this time," the communicator replied. "However, we do know that Emma Cookson was studying the Pellian planet surface for her Geography homework when her ship malfunctioned. She had to make an emergency landing."

And the communicator replayed Emma's last desperate message.

"Zach, I'm going to the Council building," Mum said, worried. "We'll have a meeting to see what we can do about getting Emma back."

And with that, Mum rushed out of the house.

Zach walked across the room in a daze. On a shelf was the holograph of him and Emma with their families on Zola-8, the leisure planet. There he was with Emma, enjoying a ride on a Zolian horse's back.

Zach's heart started to hammer. Emma was his best friend. And she was in danger... What could he do? He had to do something. He couldn't just sit around and wait for the grown-ups to sort it out.

Then he had a brilliant idea! He quickly pulled on his spacesuit and ran out into the back garden. There was his mum and dad's spaceship! He wasn't meant to use it by himself without permission. And even then he was only allowed to use it to visit certain planets – and Pellia *wasn't* one of them. But he wasn't going to let that stop him. Zach

climbed into the ship and closed the hatch. He sat in the pilot's seat and fastened his safety belt.

"Computer on," said Zach.

"Computer on!" the spaceship's computer replied.

"Emma's trapped on the planet Pellia, but she managed to send a distress message back to Earth before she was taken prisoner," Zach explained to the computer. "Can you take me to where her message came from?"

"I cannot be exact, but I *can* take you to within half a kilometre of Emma's last recorded position," said the computer.

"Then set course for the planet Pellia," said Zach firmly. "I'm going to rescue Emma myself!"

Chapter

Trapped!

Zach's spaceship landed with a THUMP on the planet's surface.

"Computer, is the air on Pellia safe for me to breathe without a space mask?" asked Zach.

"It is," the computer replied.

Zach undid his safety belt and then opened the hatch.

"Now to find Emma!" he said.

Zach walked down the steps of his spaceship and looked around. He was in a forest. It looked calm and peaceful but even so, something wasn't quite right... Zach shook his head. He'd never find Emma if he started imagining things. Taking a deep breath, he started walking.

SMACK! Zach walked straight into an invisible force field. He wanted to rub his sore nose and his bruised knees, but he couldn't move any part of his body. The force field was like an invisible wall all around him. It squeezed him so tightly that he couldn't even wriggle his fingers.

"Ha! We have you now!" A Pellian stepped out from behind a tree nearby, and came running up to Zach. A second Pellian, who looked exactly the same as the first, appeared from behind a bush and came running over as well.

"Let me out of here!" Zach demanded.

"Why should we?" asked the first Pellian.

"That's just the question I was going to ask, Pludd!" his brother Plidd said. "Yeah! Why should we?"

"Because I haven't done anything to you. I'm here to rescue my friend Emma," said Zach. "Please let me out."

Pludd and Plidd stepped back and whispered to each other for a few moments. Zach tried to listen, but he couldn't make out what they were saying.

"We'll let you go – but only if you solve our puzzle first. Isn't that right, Plidd?" said Pludd.

"You tell him, Pludd!" said Plidd.

"I can't do much trapped in here," Zach said. "Let me out and then I'll do it – I promise."

Zach didn't want to spend another second in the force field. It was horrible. He could just about breathe and speak, but that was it.

"No! Solve our puzzle first," Pludd and

Plidd started jumping up and down. "You have to solve our puzzle first."

Zach scowled at Plidd and Pludd but he knew he didn't have any choice.

"OK. What is it?" he asked.

"We're identical twins…" Pludd began. "Identical in every way…"

"Except for ten titchy-teeny-tiny-tiddly differences," Plidd grinned.

"If you spot all ten, we'll let you go," said Pludd.

"But you won't be able to do it – no one's ever managed all ten before," said Plidd.

"And what happens if I don't spot all ten?" frowned Zach.

"Then you'll be a prisoner in our force field – *forever*," the twins grinned.

Zach gasped. He couldn't believe it. He'd

come all the way from Earth to rescue Emma.
Now he was the one who needed rescuing!

"Ten differences…ten differences…" Zach
studied Pludd and Plidd carefully. He had to
find ten differences – and fast!

Chapter 5

The Draka Monsters

The moment Zach spotted the tenth difference between Pludd and Plidd, the force field crackled and disappeared.

"You two ought to be ashamed of yourselves," said Zach. "That's no way to treat visitors to your planet."

"We were just having a bit of fun, weren't we Pludd?" Plidd said to his brother.

"Yeah! Just a bit of fun," Pludd agreed.

"D'you two know where my friend Emma is? Was it you two who captured her?" asked Zach.

"Us?" said Plidd.

"No way," said Pludd. "Your friend landed on top of King Pecan's floating mansion! She'll be stuck up in that mansion for good, now, as the king's prisoner. And don't try to see him because the king is despicably mean, and he doesn't see anyone."

"Why not?" Zach asked.

"Because he doesn't like anyone," Plidd began.

"So no one likes him," Pludd finished. "He's unfriendly and bad-tempered and nasty. The nastiest Pellian on the planet."

Zach swallowed hard. The king didn't sound

like someone he wanted to meet, but he couldn't let that stop him. If Emma was stuck in the king's floating mansion, then he'd have to find a way of getting her out.

"Where can I find King Pecan?" Zach asked.

"Come with us," said Pludd and Plidd.

The two Pellians led Zach to the edge of the forest. Far away in the distance, Zach could see a house which seemed to be hanging in mid-air. Zach wondered how he'd be able to climb up to it. But he had a bigger, more immediate problem to sort out first. Ahead of him, he could hear all kinds of growling and roaring and loud, belching noises!

"Which way should I go?" asked Zach.

"You can follow that path," said Pludd, pointing to his left.

"Or that path," said Plidd, pointing to his right.

"Or that path!" Pludd and Plidd both pointed to a path in the middle.

"And of course there are a lot more paths to follow once you get going," Pludd said with delight.

"And caverns…"

"And bridges…"

"And secret passages…"

"So you'd better choose the right path or you'll run into the Draka monsters, and they eat humans!" said Plidd.

And with that, they both ran off.

Dismayed, Zach stuck his fingers in his ears. But it didn't help. He could still hear the Draka monsters roaring and howling ahead

of him. In the distance was the king's floating mansion. But which path should he take to get there?

Chapter

Seventeen Keys For Seventeen Locks

"I'm glad I got through that safely!" said Zach, dusting himself off.

Now that he was passed the Draka monsters, Zach felt that he was ready for anything! He was a lot closer to the king's floating mansion now. It bobbed gently up and down in the distance like a gigantic balloon without a string.

"How on Pellia do I get up there?" Zach asked himself.

He raced towards the floating mansion. He

was almost there, when ZWAP! Without warning, a pair of the strangest doors Zach had ever seen appeared out of nowhere. They stood upright directly under the floating mansion, but there was nothing holding them up – at least nothing that Zach could see. Cautiously, Zach tip-toed up to them. He checked on either side of the doors, but there was nothing but grass and flowers and fresh air around them!

And it wasn't just their shape that was odd, although that was strange enough, but Zach had never seen so many bolts and locks and padlocks on two doors before. He could pull back the bolts, but everything else was locked. Zach searched around for a key, but he couldn't find one.

What should I do? Zach wondered. He couldn't give up. Not now that he was so close.

"Hello? Is anyone up there?" Zach tilted his head back, and called out at the top of his voice.

Way above his head, he heard the sound of a window being pushed up. The head of an old, old Pellian with a long blue beard looked out of the window.

"What d'you want?" the old Pellian snapped

from above.

"Excuse me, but how do I get up there?" Zach called out.

"Open those doors, and then you can come up," the Pellian shouted back.

"But there's no key," Zach said.

"There are seventeen keys. Seventeen locks means seventeen keys," said the Pellian, crossly.

"Could you throw them down then, please?" asked Zach.

"You must be joking!" barked the Pellian. "I don't have the keys and even if I did, I wouldn't give them to you."

"Why not?"

"Because I don't want any visitors! I don't like visitors," answered the old Pellian.

"Are you King Pecan?" Zach asked.

"Mind your own business," said the Pellian, tapping his two noses alternately.

Zach sighed. He wasn't getting very far. He was certain that the Pellian above him was the king, but that didn't do him much good – not with the king way above in his floating mansion, and Zach firmly on the ground.

"Where do I find the seventeen keys, then?" Zach asked.

"Here, there and everywhere. But don't bother looking for them because you won't find them," the old Pellian replied.

"Couldn't you at least give me some clues?" Zach asked.

"No!" snapped the old Pellian. "I've said far too much already. Go away!"

And with that, the old Pellian pulled his head back in, like a tortoise in its shell, and slammed the window shut!

'Where do I find those keys?' Zach asked himself.

Then he remembered that he'd seen a key quite close to his spaceship.

"Oh no! I must have passed all seventeen keys on my way here," Zach realised, dismayed. "I'll have to go right back to my ship and try to find them."

If Zach didn't find the seventeen keys to fit the seventeen locks then that would be it. He'd never get to see the king. And more importantly, he'd never rescue Emma. Zach turned around and started retracing his steps. He'd have to look closely at everything he passed to find those seventeen keys.

Chapter

The Real Emma

Zach had to walk all the way back to his spaceship, then all the way back to the floating mansion, but it was worth it. He found all seventeen keys.

The moment Zach had turned the seventeenth key in the seventeenth lock, the doors creaked slowly open.

"These doors must lead somewhere," Zach muttered. "All doors lead somewhere. Otherwise what's the point of having a door in the first place?"

Zach had barely stepped through the now open doors before they clanged shut behind him. The walls of a lift suddenly appeared out of nowhere. On one wall of the lift was a very strange diagram of letters and boxes with the words 'FILL ME IN!' above it.

"Take me up to see the king, please," Zach said to the lift.

Nothing happened. Zach took a closer look at the diagram. The lift obviously wasn't going to budge until he worked out which letter fitted in each box.

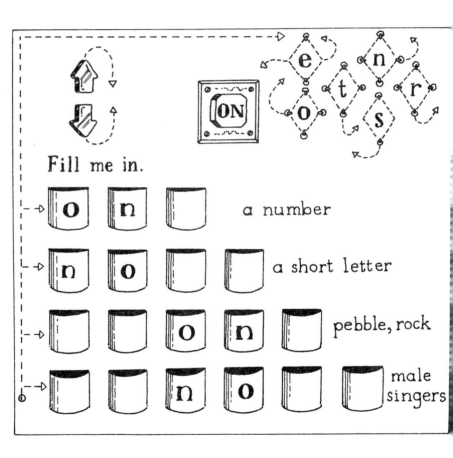

Fill me in.

o n ☐ — a number

n o ☐ ☐ — a short letter

☐ ☐ o n ☐ — pebble, rock

☐ ☐ n o ☐ ☐ — male singers

The moment Zach filled in the last letter, he was whizzed straight up into the air. It happened so quickly he almost fell over. Up and up and up he went, getting closer and closer to the floating mansion.

As the lift approached the mansion, a hole appeared in the bottom of the building, and the lift carried on rising. The hole closed under Zach, and he found himself in the hall of the mansion.

Zach looked around. He didn't like the look of it at all. It was dark and gloomy and full of cobwebs and long shadows. And it was so quiet, Zach could hear himself breathing.

The old Pellian who'd been at the window earlier appeared at the top of the stairs, and slid down the banisters towards Zach. He now wore a crown and a long flowing robe.

"I knew you were the king," Zach said.

"Who are you? And how did you manage to find all seventeen keys to my lift?" scowled King Pecan. "No one's ever done that before."

"I'm Zach, and I've come to rescue my friend Emma," said Zach.

"You can't have her back," said the king. "If you take her back to your planet, who will I have to talk to?"

"You can't kidnap people just so you'll have someone to chat to!" Zach frowned. "You've got to let Emma go. I'm not going home without her."

King Pecan and Zach eyed each other warily.

"I'll tell you what…" smiled King Pecan slowly. "Emma's in that room over there. If you can find her, I'll let you both go back to Earth."

Hhmm! Zach didn't like the sly gleam in the king's eyes at all.

"What's the catch?" Zach asked, suspiciously.

"There's no catch," said the king. "Just go and find her."

King Pecan opened the door to the room on his left. Then he beckoned to Zach to follow him.

Zach stepped into the room, then gasped. And no wonder! The room was full of Emmas! No matter which way Zach turned, all he could see was row upon row of Emmas.

"None of the Emmas in this room can speak to you so don't bother to ask them questions, but don't let that stop you," the king grinned. "Find the real Emma and I promise I'll let both of you leave. Otherwise you'll both be my prisoners for ever."

Dazed, Zach wandered around the room. Each Emma looked the same to him. How would he ever find the real one?

Chapter

King Pecan's Mystery

The moment Zach laid his hand on the real Emma's shoulder, all the other Emmas vanished.

"Zach! Thank goodness! I was worried you might get it wrong," Emma breathed a sigh of relief.

"No way! I know you too well," Zach turned to the king. "I've done it! Now keep your promise, and let us leave."

"No, I won't! I won't! Emma's the first person I've spoken to in ages," said King Pecan.

"But there are plenty of Pellians on this planet to talk to," said Zach.

"How can I speak to them when I'm stuck up here, and they're all down on the ground? It's hard to have a proper conversation when you have to shout all the time," sniffed the king. "And no one ever comes up to my mansion for a chat."

"I came to your mansion and you didn't want to speak to me. You told me to go away," Zach pointed out.

"That's because I knew you'd come to take Emma away," answered King Pecan. "And we were just in the middle of a game of *Scrabble*."

In spite of King Pecan's bad behaviour, Zach felt a bit sorry for him.

"Why don't you just use your lift and go

down to the ground?" Zach asked.

"I can't. I've tried and tried, but it won't work with me in it. It works for everyone else, except me. I'm all alone and lonely."

"There must be some way of getting you down to the ground," said Emma.

"It can't be done. I can't get down unless my whole mansion goes down to the ground as well," said King Pecan.

Zach and Emma looked at each other.

"How on Pellia do we do that?" Emma asked.

"There's one way to do it," the king began reluctantly. "On a wall in my dining room, there's an ancient mystery. If I could only solve that mystery then I'd know how to land my mansion, but I've never been able to work it out."

"Let's all take a look," Zach suggested.

"Maybe with all three of us working together we'll be able to sort it out."

"You won't be able to do it. It's too hard," said King Pecan. "My great-great-great-great grandfather loved to study your planet Earth and he's the one who invented this mystery. I don't know what most of the things in it are."

"At least let us try," said Zach.

"Oh, all right then," said the king without much enthusiasm. "Follow me."

Zach and Emma followed the king to his dining room. They both stared when they saw King Pecan's mystery. It covered one entire wall of the dining room and the dining room was HUGE! All three of them moved in for a closer look. High above the mystery was written the words:

To come down to Pellia follow these instructions...

"Well, the first picture is a squirrel, the second picture is a trestle..." Emma frowned.

"The third picture is an apple..." added Zach.

"But what does it mean?" asked the king.

The king, Emma and Zach walked up and down looking at all the different pictures on the wall.

"I've got it! I've got it!" said Zach. "We have to take the first letter of each word and then spell out the new words that we make."

"You're right!" said Emma. "Let's work out
what all the pictures are first. Then we can see

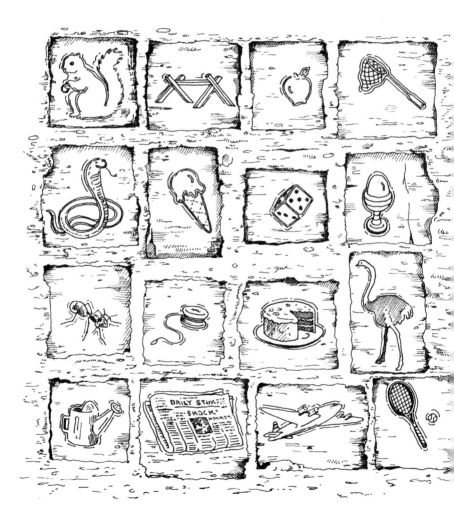

what the new message says."

Chapter

Down to Pellia and Back to Earth

"The message says 'Stand outside and say "come down at once"'," Zach said, when at last they'd all worked it out.

"We'll go down in the lift and say it. You'll be down on the ground in no time, your majesty," said Emma.

Zach and Emma ran to the lift and took it down on the ground. King Pecan looked out of the window.

"Good luck!" he shouted.

Emma and Zach waved back.

"This is it," breathed Zach. "I'll count to three, then we'll say it. One…two…three…"

"COME DOWN AT ONCE!"

At first Emma and Zach thought that nothing was happening. Then very, very slowly, the house began to descend – a centimetre at a time.

King Pecan turned his head this way and that. "It's working! It's working!" he yelled. "Hooray!"

The mansion had barely touched the ground before the king was out of the front door and dancing around on the grass.

"I'm out! I'm free!" Overjoyed, the king danced from foot to foot to foot!

Then he looked around and stopped dancing.

"But I'm still all alone," he sighed.

"Your majesty, I have an idea. Why don't you invite all the Pellians into your mansion for a party?" Emma suggested. "Then you wouldn't be so lonely. You could have parties every day if you wanted to!"

"Hhmm!" King Pecan stroked his beard, then sighed again. "What's the point? No one likes me."

"Only because they think you don't like them," said Zach.

"And we like you, don't we Zach," Emma nudged Zach in the ribs.

"Er…yes, we do," Zach had to think about it first.

King Pecan grinned. "Really? You do! At

last! Someone likes me!"

"And we'll come back to Pellia and visit you just as often as we can," Emma said.

Zach nodded. "But only if you promise not to kidnap anyone else."

"I promise," said King Pecan immediately.

King Pecan followed Emma's advice and opened up his palace to all the people of Pellia. He had a big party for everyone in the kingdom and invited Zach and Emma to be the guests-of-honour.

"I'm afraid we can't, your majesty," Zach said, eyeing the mountains of food with regret. "We have to get back home."

"Why don't I load up your ship with some of our Pellian delicacies?" the king suggested. "That way you won't miss out."

Zach and Emma grinned at each other.

"What a good idea!" they both said at once.

So, as Emma's ship still wasn't working, King Pecan had Zach's ship loaded up with all kinds of Pellian goodies.

There was Pellian Surprise which was Zach's favourite. It started off tasting of scampi and chips, and then turned into double-double chocolate chip ice-cream in your mouth. And there were marmalade jellies and sausage-flavoured lollies and Pellian Punch to wash it all down. Pellian Punch was special; it started off tasting of cranberries, then blueberries, blackberries, raspberries and strawberries, in that order.

Emma and Zach climbed into Zach's spaceship and waved goodbye to the Pellians.

"We'll be back soon, your majesty," Emma called and waved, before closing the hatch.

Emma and Zach strapped themselves into their seats.

"Computer on," said Zach.

"Computer on," the computer replied.

"Set course for home," said Zach.

Once the spaceship took off, Emma said, "Thanks for coming to get me, Zach."

"No problem," Zach smiled. "Besides, it was only fair. After all, you rescued me when I got trapped in the undersea world on Planet Ullio! Remember?"

"I remember! That was hard work!" Emma nodded vigorously. "Do your mum and dad know that you came to rescue me?"

"Nah!" Zach shook his head. "All the grown-ups are probably still having a meeting about how to get you back to Earth. We'll be home before they even realise that I went! And just in time for dinner."

"You're not going to have your dinner when we get home," said Emma, aghast. "Not on top of all this food! You couldn't!"

"Just watch me!" Zach grinned. "Rescuing you has really built up an appetite!"

ANSWERS

Chapter 2:

Chapter 3:

Chapter 4:

Chapter 5:

1st Puzzle:

ON —> ONE —> NOTE —>
STONE —> TENORS

Chapter 5:
2nd Puzzle:

Chapter 6

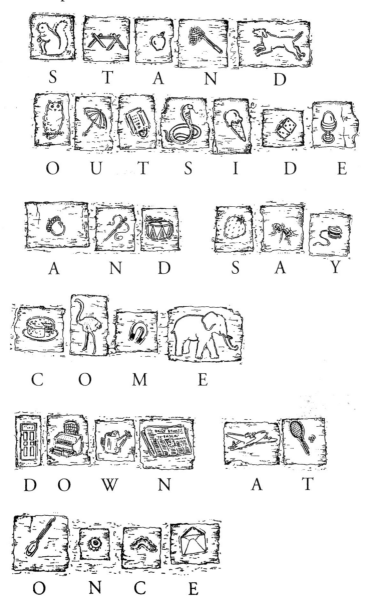

S T A N D

O U T S I D E

A N D   S A Y

C O M E

D O W N   A T

O N C E